Remembering with love,
Mr. Christmas,
Freddy Faust
(1947–2005)
—J.M.

For Edward Emilio Vidal
—W.W.

Text copyright © 2005 by Jean Marzollo.
Photographs copyright © 1992 by Walter Wick.

All rights reserved. Published by Scholastic Inc.
SCHOLASTIC, CARTWHEEL BOOKS, and associated logos
are trademarks and/or registered trademarks of Scholastic Inc.
Lexile is a registered trademark of MetaMetrics, Inc.

All images by Walter Wick taken from *I Spy Christmas*.
Published by Scholastic Inc. in 1992.

Library of Congress Cataloging-in-Publication Data
Marzollo, Jean.
I spy Santa Claus / riddles by Jean Marzollo; photographs by Walter Wick.
    p. cm. — (Scholastic reader. Level 1)
"Cartwheel books."
ISBN 0-439-78414-X (pbk.)
1. Picture puzzles — Juvenile literature. 2. Santa Claus — Juvenile literature.
I. Wick, Walter, ill. II. Title. III. Series.
GV1507.P47M295 2006
793.73 — dc22

ISBN-13: 978-0-439-78414-6
ISBN-10: 0-439-78414-X

10 9 8   08 09 10

Printed in the U.S.A. 23 • This edition first printing, May 2008

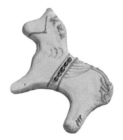

BEGINNING READER
LEVEL 1
50-250 WORDS

I SPY

SANTA CLAUS

Riddles by Jean Marzollo
Photographs by Walter Wick

Cartwheel
·B·O·O·K·S·®

SCHOLASTIC INC.
New York   Toronto   London   Auckland   Sydney
Mexico City   New Delhi   Hong Kong   Buenos Aires

I spy

a belt,

a bell that's blue,

a teddy bear's bow,

and a butterfly, too.

I spy

an umbrella,

yarn that's pink,

Santa on skis,

 and a nice warm drink.

I spy

a dog,

 a marble that's red,

a Santa cap bear,

and a heart-shaped head.

I spy

 two horses,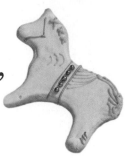

a cookie O,

 a purple squirrel,

and a star's yellow glow.

I spy

a white horse,

 a 7,

two socks,

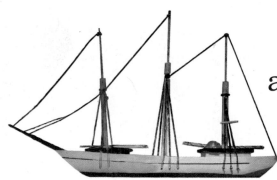 a sailing ship,

and a furry white fox.

I spy

a trumpet,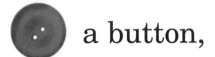

a button,

a jack,

 a bearded face,

and a nose that's black.

I spy

a carrot,

 the number 8,

a bear on a drum,

 and a roller skate.

I spy

glasses,

a wooden pan,

an empty heart,

and a big policeman.

I spy

a dog,

twin birds,

a fish,

a toothy grin,

and a star for a wish.

I spy

 a rooster,

Santa in the sky,

a gift,

and an angel ready to fly.

I spy two matching words.

 Santa cap bear

two socks

Santa in the sky

I spy two matching words.

dog

dog

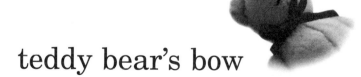

teddy bear's bow

I spy two words that start with the letter P.

big policeman

 yarn that's pink

cookie O

I spy two words that start with the letters GL.

glasses

sailing ship

star's yellow glow

I spy two words that end with the letter T.

trumpet

 carrot

furry white fox

I spy two words that end with the letters EL.

 purple squirrel

jack

 angel ready to fly

I spy two words that rhyme.

 marble that's red

 fish

heart-shaped head

I spy two words that rhyme.

 two horses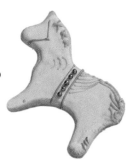

bell that's blue

 gift